For Rea (and her new home)
- S. C.

For my family and good friends . . .
- C. P.

tiger tales
5 River Road, Suite 128, Wilton, CT 06897
Published in the United States 2015
Originally published in Great Britain 2015
by Little Tiger Press
Text by Suzanne Chiew
Text copyright © 2015 Little Tiger Press
Illustrations copyright © 2015 Caroline Pedler
ISBN-13: 978-1-58925-173-1
ISBN-10: 1-58925-173-3
Printed in China
LTP/1400/0995/0914

10 9 8 7 6 5 4 3 2 1

For more insight and activities,
visit us at www.tigertalesbooks.com

When You Need A Friend

by Suzanne Chiew *Illustrated by* Caroline Pedler

tiger tales®

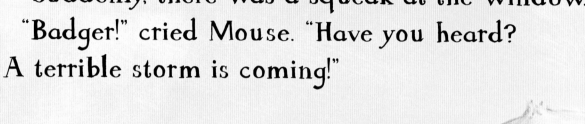

"*Mighty oaks from acorns grow!*" sang Badger
as he bustled around his cozy burrow. Tucked
beneath the roots of the old oak tree, it had
always been a happy home for badgers.

Suddenly, there was a squeak at the window.

"Badger!" cried Mouse. "Have you heard?
A terrible storm is coming!"

"A storm?" cried Rabbit, hopping up.
"My nest will blow away!" flapped Bird.
"And what about my lettuce garden?"
Hedgehog gasped. "Badger! What should
we do?"

"Don't worry!" smiled Badger. "We'll
make your homes as strong as castles!"

First, Badger made a sturdy door for Rabbit's burrow. "To keep out the wild winds!" he said.

Then, he used some overturned flowerpots to cover Hedgehog's prize lettuce . . .

and built a box
around the nest
to keep Bird safe
and dry.

"There!" sighed Badger happily, tying Mouse's ladder in place.

"Thank you, Badger!" Mouse squeaked. "Now please hurry home—the storm is almost here!"

Badger trudged back toward his old oak tree, but very soon the rain was pouring down.

"Oh, dear!" Badger frowned,
as thunder crashed and the wind
howled. "Oh, dear, oh, dear!"

Suddenly, a door flew open. "Badger!" yelled Rabbit. "You must come in from the storm!" "It is a bit blustery!" chuckled Badger, following Rabbit inside.

The baby bunnies gathered around. "Will we get blown away?" they cried. "We're quite safe here," said Badger gently. "Now, who would like a story?" And as they snuggled close, the bunnies soon forgot to be scared.

All through the night, the storm roared and raged. Thunder boomed, lightning flashed, and the animals shivered in their homes, waiting for morning to arrive.

But when the sun came up,
the friends had a terrible shock.
"Where will poor Badger live now?"
gasped Hedgehog. "There have always
been badgers under that old oak tree!"

"He can stay with me," trilled Bird, "although my nest is very high."

"Or with me," suggested Mouse, "although it might be a squeeze."

"He can share with me!" cried Hedgehog. "But we'll need a lot more leaves to snuggle beneath!"

When Badger and Rabbit arrived, their friends rushed over.

"My poor, poor house," Badger sighed sadly.

"How can we help?" squeaked Mouse.

"Yes, what can we do?" asked Hedgehog.

Badger took a deep breath. "Don't worry," he said slowly. "Every problem has a solution!"

"First let's rescue my books and gather my pans," called Badger. "Then we'll turn this grand old oak into a brand—new house!"

The friends got to work at once. There was a job for everyone, no matter how small.

For days and days, they chopped and sawed . . .

and hammered and painted . . .

until they had used every last piece of wood to build something very special . . . .

"My wonderful new home!" beamed Badger. "You're the best friends I could ever wish for!"

Just then, Hedgehog rushed over. "We forgot to use this!" he cried, holding up a tiny acorn.

"I know just what we'll do with that," said Badger. "Mighty oaks from acorns grow!"

He dug a little hole, and they planted the acorn very carefully.

And from that day on, and forever more, there were always badgers living under the new oak tree.